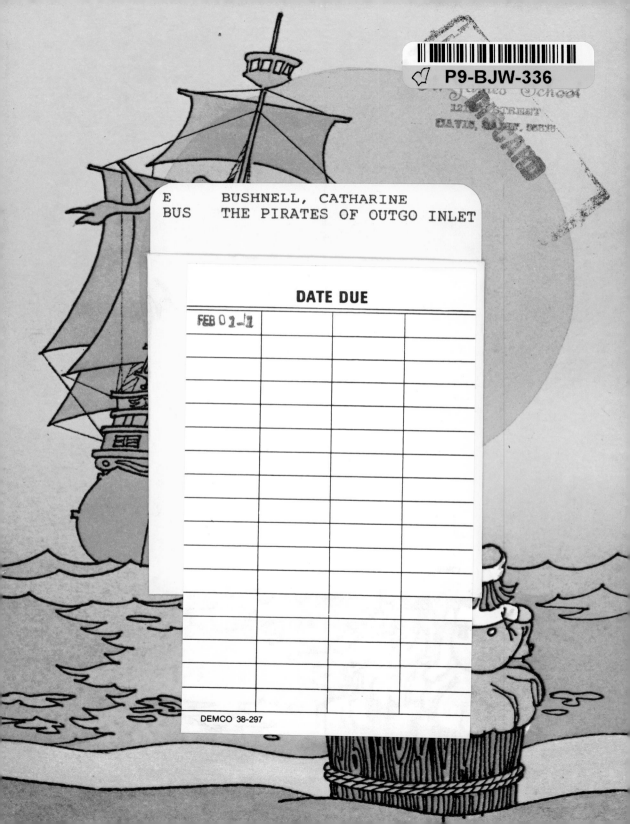

DATE DUE

FEB 0 1 - 1			

DEMCO 38-297

RAGGEDY ANN & ANDY ™
AND
THE PIRATES OF OUTGO INLET

E
BUS

by Catharine Bushnell
Illustrated by Vernon McKissack
The Bobbs-Merrill Company, Inc.
Indianapolis / New York

Based on the characters created by Johnny Gruelle.

Raggedy Ann and Raggedy Andy and all related
characters appearing in this book are trade-
marks of The Bobbs-Merrill Company, Inc.

ISBN 0-672-52689-1
Library of Congress Catalog Card Number: 80-69646
Manufactured in the United States of America

First printing

LATE ONE NIGHT aboard the pirate ship, "Harmless Fly," Captain Sniggle was reading the pirate crew a bedtime story. It was called "Famous Pirates I Have Known," by Dirty Davey.

Sniggle looked up sadly. "I wish we could be big bad pirates like they were," he said. "I wish someone would call me 'Fearsome Sniggle' or 'Sniggle the Terrible.' Sylvester Pangborn Sniggle is just not piratey enough."

Captain Sniggle went on reading. "Dirty Davey says, 'All the Old Salts of my pirate days were rough and tough. Real sea dogs. . .' " Sniggle stopped reading. "A sea dog! That's it!" he cried.

"But, Captain," said the First Mate, "Dirty Davey means. . ." "Quiet," shouted Sniggle. "Listen, men. We need a dog. We need the very best dog in the whole world. And I know where to find him. Let's go!" And he stumped out the door.

The First Mate followed him, muttering, "Not a *real* dog. 'Sea Dog' means a really tough, clever sailor." But the captain was too far ahead to hear him.

The next day, Marcella decided to have a tea party. She carried her afternoon snack and a cup of milk out to the garden table. She put Raggedy Ann and Raggedy Andy together in the chair beside her and poured pretend tea for them.

"I know that dogs don't like tea," she said to Raggedy Arthur, "so you go and run in the grass. I will give you a biscuit later."

Marcella did not see Captain Sniggle and his pirate crew. But Sniggle saw Raggedy Arthur. He clapped his hands with glee. "There is the only dog for us," he whispered. "Now we must make Marcella go away."

He picked up a small rock and threw it right into the middle of Marcella's cup. Milk splashed all over everything. "My goodness," said Marcella. "How strange. I must go clean off my shirt. You stay here, Raggedy Ann and Andy."

As soon as Marcella had gone, the pirates jumped on
Raggedy Arthur and stuffed him into a big bag.
"Oh, dear!" Raggedy Ann cried. "You leave our dog
alone!"

"He's *our* dog now, missy," shouted Sniggle. "He's
off to the high seas!" The pirates disappeared into
the woods.

"Oh, Andy, we must go after them. Poor Arthur," said Raggedy Ann. She put a handful of cookies into her pocket for later. "I think Marcella will be gone for a while. Let's hurry."

Raggedy Ann slid down the leg of the chair. Raggedy Andy followed close behind. "I'm an expert on footprints," said Andy. "I'll lead the way."

They ran for a long time. Suddenly they came over the top of a hill. The sea rolled on the beach in front of them. "Look," said Raggedy Ann sadly, "that must be the pirate ship. It is very far away. We will never catch them now."

"Rats," said Raggedy Andy. "A footprint expert is no good on water. We must think of something else."

"Here's a cookie to help you think," said Raggedy Ann.

Just then, a voice behind her said, "Is that vanilla cookies I smell? I just *love* vanilla cookies." "Oh, it's a pelican!" cried Raggedy Ann.

"That's right," said the bird. "Spike Pelican at your service. You seem to have a little problem here. By the way, can you spare a cookie?"

"Of course," said Raggedy Ann. The cookie disappeared into his giant bill. "Thank you," said Spike. "So, the pirates have taken your friend. I can take you to their hideout at Outgo Inlet. But you must promise to be very careful. They aren't really mean pirates yet. So far they haven't hurt anyone. But they are trying to learn proper pirating. You can never tell when they might get it right! Let's hurry!"

Raggedy Ann and Andy climbed into the pouch in his beak. "Yuck," said Raggedy Andy. "This place is covered with cookie crumbs."

"Be grateful, Andrew," said Ann. "Most pelicans eat fish."

"Ihs oh-ee oo ee iff-ih-kuh oo ee er I aa oh-ee ith y ow oh-eh," mumbled Spike. "What?" said Andy. "He said, 'It's going to be difficult to see where I am going with my mouth open.' That's what," said Raggedy Ann. Spike Pelican flapped his wings. They soared into the sky.

On the pirate ship, Captain Sniggle ordered, "Bring me that dog." The crew dumped Raggedy Arthur out onto the deck. He ran over to Sniggle and fastened his teeth firmly into the pirate captain's wooden leg.

"Just a moment here, dog," said Sniggle. "You don't understand. We want you to be our sea dog. You will live in the lap of luxury. We will treat you like a king. You will have your weight in sirloin steak."

Arthur's eyes lit up. But he did not let go. Raggedy Arthur is a one playroom dog.

"Very well," said Captain Sniggle. "I tried to be
nice. Clap him in irons, men!" "But, Captain," cried
the First Mate, "I wouldn't do that to a dog. Besides,
he's got your leg."

"Never mind about that. Put the chains on him!"
bellowed the Captain. "Full speed ahead to our
Outgo Inlet hideout!"

Spike Pelican landed gently on the sand. "This is Outgo Inlet," he said. "That shack is the pirates' hideout. If you hurry, you will be there before they are. But be careful."

"We will, Spike," said Raggedy Ann. "Here is another cookie. Thank you for your help." She waved good-bye to the bird.

Raggedy Ann and Andy ran to the bushes beside the
old run-down shack. "Boy," said Andy, "this place
sure is a dump. I thought pirates lived better than
this. Oops! Look out, here they come!" He and Raggedy Ann ducked out of sight.

Captain Sniggle came first, loudly pleading, "Be reasonable, can't you?" At first, Raggedy Ann and Andy thought he was talking to his foot. But then they saw their own Raggedy Arthur. His teeth were still firmly fastened to the Captain's peg leg.

"Oooh, that horrible man," said Raggedy Ann. "Do you think if we asked nicely, he would let Arthur go?" "Not a chance," said Andy. "He didn't ask nicely when he took our dog."

Inside the hideout, Sniggle stood very still. "Did you hear anything?" he whispered. "Harry, you and Peewee go and check."

Raggedy Andy set his cap. "We'll just have to *make* him give Raggedy Arthur back." He stood up bravely and picked up a very large stick. He walked around the corner.

"Hello," said Harry. "Hello," said Peewee. "Why don't you come in?" said Harry. "And bring your sister," said Peewee. Andy looked at Raggedy Ann. They were captured.

Harry pushed Raggedy Ann and Raggedy Andy
through the door. "Well, well," Sniggle said. "I see
that you have come to rescue your dog. You are too
late. Dirty Davey says we need a sea dog. Arthur is
our sea dog now. Even if he doesn't want to be."

"But, Captain," said the First Mate. "Quiet, Perkins!"
Sniggle roared. "You men bring out the vat!"

Two pirates rolled out the big wooden tub that they used for taking baths on Saturday nights. Now, it was filled to the rim with steaming hot sea water. The pirates' hands were crusty-white with dried salt.

"Pitch the pup into the drink!" cried Sniggle. "When he dries, he will be a really salty sea dog."

"Raggedy Arthur doesn't like baths at all. Not even in Marcella's sink at home," said Raggedy Ann. "He would just hate a salty bath. Besides, he has that big chain on. He will sink to the bottom and get waterlogged. Then you will have a soggy dog."

Captain Sniggle thought for a moment. "You have a
point, Raggedy Ann," he said. "Take off his chain.
But don't let him escape."

The Second Mate took the chain off. Arthur looked
at First Mate Perkins. He remembered how Perkins
had tried to stop Sniggle from chaining him. He
wanted to say thank you. So, Arthur let go of the
Captain's leg, and licked the First Mate's face all
over.

Perkins was indeed a dog lover. But Perkins was also very ticklish. He dropped Raggedy Arthur and rolled on the floor laughing.

"You idiot!" shouted the Captain. "Catch that dog, men!" All the pirates ran around the room after Raggedy Arthur. Raggedy Ann and Andy were left unguarded.

Andy shouted, "Come on, Arthur!" The three of them ran out the door. The pirates all ran after them. The pirates ran faster. The Raggedies were soon surrounded.

"Please, Captain," cried Raggedy Ann, "our play-room would be empty and sad without Arthur. Don't take him away."

"I don't mean to make you sad," the Captain snuffled. "Oh, bother." "BUT, CAPTAIN!" Perkins shouted, "I have been trying to tell you! 'Sea dog' is only a nickname for a really tough old sailor. It isn't a real dog at all!"

"Oh," said Sniggle; and "Oh," said Sniggle again. "I made a terrible mistake. We're not really right for pirating, I guess. But we do love sailing. And wearing shiny medals."

"Well, then," said Raggedy Ann. "Why don't you join the Navy? Then you can sail. That would be a better job than pirating."

"Admirable idea!" cried Sniggle. "Then I don't have to wear this awful peg leg any more." He unstrapped the leg. His own leg came down from behind him. He rubbed his knee.

"We will join the Navy today," he said. "But first, we will take you back to Marcella's garden.

The Raggedies got back just in time. Marcella was coming out of the house. "Did you have a good time playing in the grass?" she asked Arthur.

Suddenly she saw an odd-shaped piece of wood near him. "That's funny," she said. "That wasn't here before. And it seems to have teeth marks in it. I wonder where it came from."

But Arthur just sat there smiling. And when Marcella picked him up, he winked at Raggedy Ann and Raggedy Andy.